Best Wishes —
Margo Shpachow
90

B·A·B·A

written and illustrated
by
Tanya Shpakow

ALFRED A. KNOPF 🐕 NEW YORK

For my parents,
Tom and Sharon Shpakow

THIS IS A BORZOI BOOK
PUBLISHED BY ALFRED A. KNOPF, INC.

Copyright © 1989 by Tanya Shpakow.
All rights reserved under International and Pan-American Copyright
Conventions. Published in the United States by Alfred A. Knopf, Inc.,
New York, and simultaneously in Canada by Random House of
Canada Limited, Toronto. Distributed by Random House, Inc., New York.
Manufactured in the United States of America
Book design by Elizabeth Hardie

2 4 6 8 0 9 7 5 3 1

Library of Congress Cataloging-in-Publication Data
Shpakow, Tanya. Baba. Summary: A little girl, convinced her
Russian grandmother is magical, sneaks into her
large bag one evening to find out where
"Baba" goes every Monday night.
ISBN 0-394-89802-8
ISBN 0-394-99802-2 (lib. bdg.)
[1. Grandmothers—Fiction] I. Title.
PZ7.S559144Bab 1989 [E] 88-8223

Many years ago, in the windiest part of Old Russia, a little girl-baby was born. She was sold to the Gypsies for a penny.

They taught her how to sing...how to dance...and how to slip in and out of places without a sound.

The girl-baby grew up and grew old. Now she is my grandmother. I call her Baba.

At night Baba tells me stories she heard long, long ago. She knows about magic. She says in the old days the Gypsies could fly—even the babies!

On windy days the lightest Gypsies were fastened to the ground with string and yarn. But sometimes accidents happened...

and I think that's how Baba came to America!

My friends all laugh when they see me with Baba. They pretend to be too grown-up to believe in magic.

But I know better.

Baba has big black shoes that never wear out. Even on muddy days they stay shiny.

Every Monday night she slips away. All she takes is her knitting bag. When I ask her to take me along, she says, "No place for children!"

When she comes home, she empties her pockets and unpacks her knitting bag. Sometimes there's a present for me. Baba has secrets!

I'm sure she visits the Gypsies!

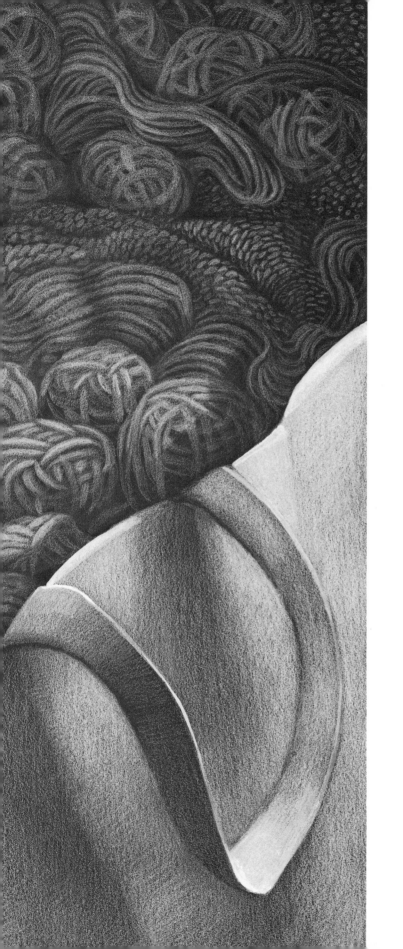

And I have a secret too.

Tonight I'm going with her.

Baba lifts the bag with me
in it!

We bump up and down
in the nighttime wind.
Overhead, leaves twirl like
bats. Red-hot sparks light
the sky. A curtain of smoke
slides all around us....

We're *flying*!

We land in a lighted place.

Baba sets the bag down
with a thump. Music is
playing. Steamy heat makes
the air thick as warm velvet.
I crouch low and listen....
I hear Baba laugh.

The Gypsies are nearby!

Bumblebee voices buzz around me. Broken bits of words whistle past my ears. A scream cuts through the air like a sharp knife! Shouts shake the floor.

"Magic!" I whisper. I jump up to see....

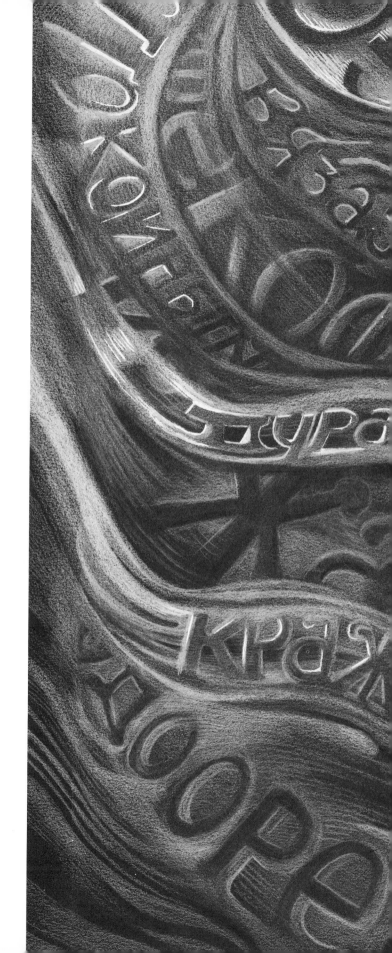

The room becomes still. A hundred feet in big black shoes stand silently. A cane raps in rhythm.

I look up and *they* look down.

I don't see Baba.

Without saying anything, Baba takes my hand.

"Where is the magic?" I ask. "Where are the Gypsies?"
But Baba isn't listening. She pulls me through the crowd.
"No place for children!" she says.

Howls of laughter roll down the steps after us.
My eyes sting. I bite my lip. I turn back to look....

I stare at the sign. A bingo game?

Baba asks me what is wrong. But I won't answer.

She isn't magic! She can't fly!

Baba takes me home.

At home I hide.

Baba starts to tell me a story. After a while I crawl out. Maybe magic doesn't matter much....

I climb into bed, close to Baba. She kisses me and sings me a lullaby. Her foot taps softly. My eyes begin to close. And then I remember...

those big black shoes never wear out!

Baba has secrets.

She stands in the shadows. Her coat is buttoned and her scarf is tied tight. The knitting bag is nearby. I wonder if she is waiting for me to go to sleep?

I try to stay awake, but my
eyes won't stay open....

"Good night, Baba."

"Good night."